There Was an
OLD LADY

Retold by STEVEN ANDERSON
Illustrated by LUKE FLOWERS

CANTATA
LEARNING

WWW.CANTATALEARNING.COM

CANTATA LEARNING

Published by Cantata Learning
1710 Roe Crest Drive
North Mankato, MN 56003
www.cantatalearning.com

Library of Congress Control Number: 2015932810
Anderson, Steven
    There Was an Old Lady / retold by Steven Anderson; Illustrated by Luke
Flowers
    Series: Sing-along Silly Songs
    Audience: Ages: 3–8; Grades: PreK–3
    Summary: In this classic song, an old lady swallows some hard-to-believe
things, starting with a fly.
    ISBN: 978-1-63290-382-2 (library binding/CD)
    ISBN: 978-1-63290-513-0 (paperback/CD)
    ISBN: 978-1-63290-543-7 (paperback)
    1. Stories in rhyme. 2. Animals (Farm)—fiction.

Book design and art direction, Tim Palin Creative
Editorial direction, Flat Sole Studio
Music direction, Elizabeth Draper
Music arranged and produced by Musical Youth Productions

Printed in the United States of America in North Mankato, Minnesota.
122015   0326CGS16

ACCESS THE MUSIC!

SCAN CODE WITH MOBILE APP

CANTATALEARNING.COM

Have you ever heard about the old lady who **swallowed** a fly? That's not the only animal she ate! The old lady also **gulped** down a spider and a bird and many other animals to try and catch that fly.

To find out what happened, turn the page and sing along!

5

There was an old lady who swallowed a fly.

I don't know why she swallowed the fly.
Perhaps she'll cry.

7

There was an old lady who swallowed a spider that wiggled and wiggled and tickled inside her.

She swallowed the spider to catch the fly.
I don't know why she swallowed the fly.
Perhaps she'll cry.

9

There was an old lady who swallowed a bird.
How **absurd** to swallow a bird!

She swallowed the bird to catch the spider that wiggled and wiggled and tickled inside her. She swallowed the spider to catch the fly. I don't know why she swallowed the fly. Perhaps she'll cry.

There was an old lady who swallowed a cat.
Imagine that! She swallowed a cat.

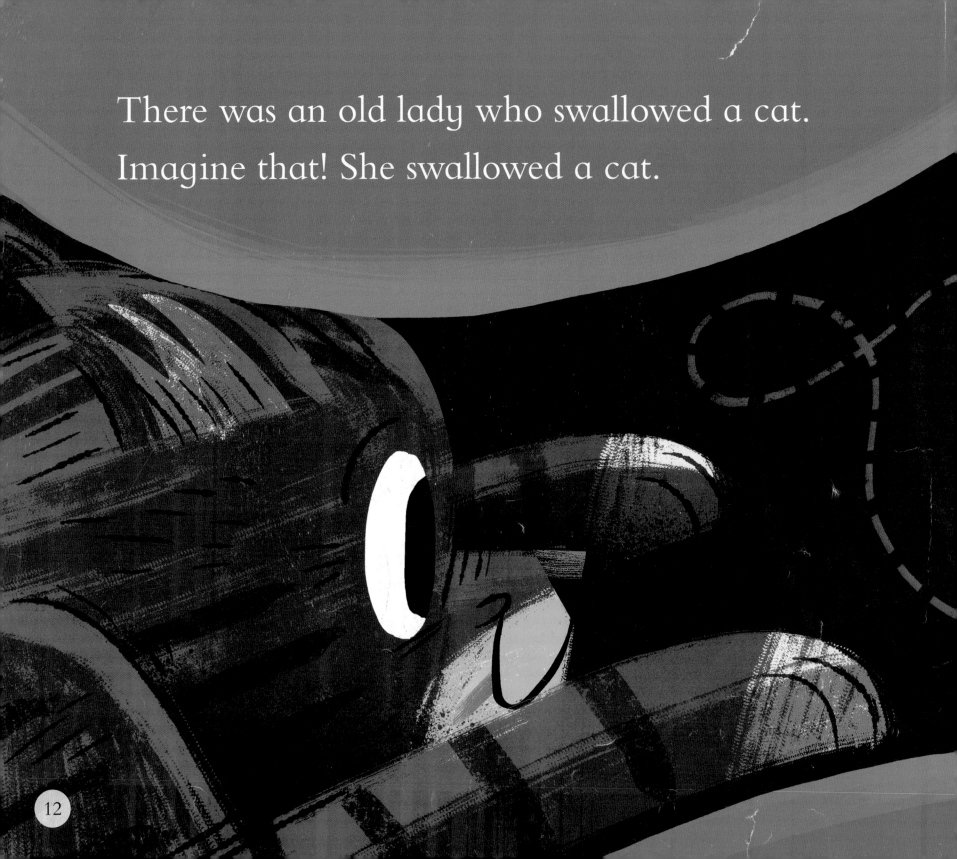

She swallowed the dog to catch the cat.

She swallowed the cat to catch the bird.

She swallowed the bird to catch the spider
that wiggled and wiggled and tickled inside her.

She swallowed the spider to catch the fly.

I don't know why she swallowed the fly.

Perhaps she'll cry.

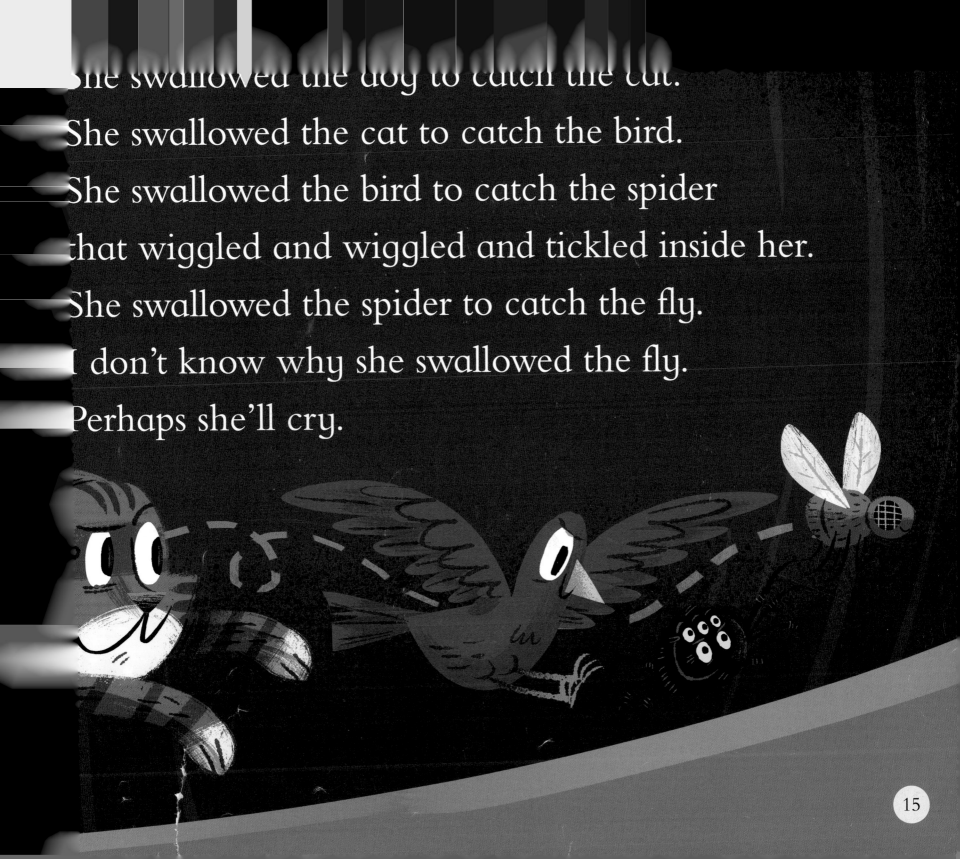

There was an old lady who swallowed a goat—
just opened her throat and swallowed a goat!

She swallowed the goat to catch the dog.

She swallowed the dog to catch the cat.

She swallowed the cat to catch the bird.

She swallowed the bird to catch the spider
that wiggled and wiggled and tickled inside her.

She swallowed the spider to catch the fly.

But I don't know why she swallowed that fly.

Perhaps she'll cry.

There was an old lady who swallowed a cow.
I don't know how she swallowed a cow!

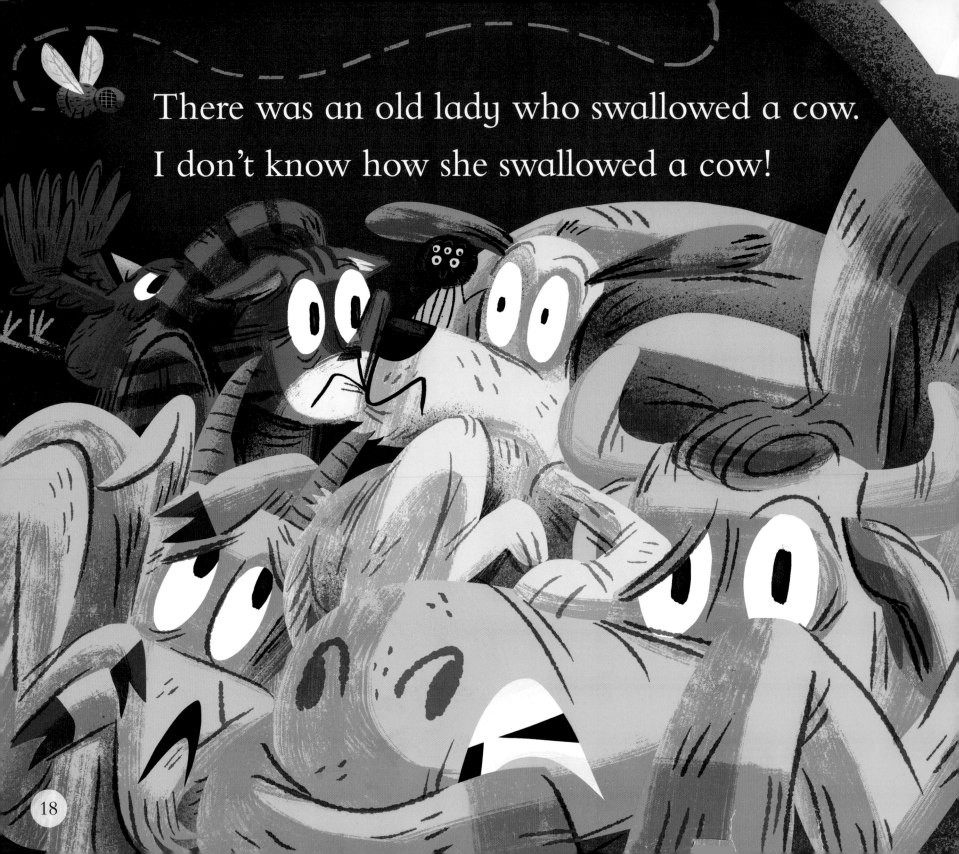

She swallowed the cow to catch the goat.

She swallowed the goat to catch the dog.

She swallowed the dog to catch the cat.

She swallowed the cat to catch the bird.

She swallowed the bird to catch the spider
that wiggled and wiggled and tickled inside her.

She swallowed the spider to catch the fly.

But I don't know why she swallowed that fly.

Perhaps she'll cry.

20

There was an old lady who swallowed a horse.
She cried, "Wait! A horse?"
She didn't, of course.

21

SONG LYRICS
There Was an Old Lady

There was an old lady who swallowed
a fly.

I don't know why she swallowed the fly.
Perhaps she'll cry.

There was an old lady who swallowed
a spider
that wiggled and wiggled and tickled
inside her.

She swallowed the spider to catch the fly.
I don't know why she swallowed the fly.
Perhaps she'll cry.

There was an old lady who swallowed
a bird.
How absurd to swallow a bird!

She swallowed the bird to catch the spider
that wiggled and wiggled and tickled
inside her.
She swallowed the spider to catch the fly.
I don't know why she swallowed the fly.
Perhaps she'll cry.

There was an old lady who swallowed
a cat.
Imagine that! She swallowed a cat.

She swallowed the cat to catch the bird.
She swallowed the bird to catch the spider
that wiggled and wiggled and tickled
inside her.
She swallowed the spider to catch the fly.
I don't know why she swallowed the fly.
Perhaps she'll cry.

There was an old lady who swallowed
a dog.
My, what a hog, to swallow a dog.

She swallowed the dog to catch the cat.
She swallowed the cat to catch the bird.
She swallowed the bird to catch the spider
that wiggled and wiggled and tickled
inside her.
She swallowed the spider to catch the fly.
I don't know why she swallowed the fly.
Perhaps she'll cry.

There was an old lady who swallowed
a goat—
just opened her throat and swallowed
a goat!

She swallowed the goat to catch the dog.
She swallowed the dog to catch the cat.
She swallowed the cat to catch the bird.
She swallowed the bird to catch the spider
that wiggled and wiggled and tickled
inside her.

She swallowed the spider to catch the fly.
But I don't know why she swallowed
that fly.
Perhaps she'll cry.

There was an old lady who swallowed
a cow.
I don't know how she swallowed a cow!

She swallowed the cow to catch the goat.
She swallowed the goat to catch the dog.
She swallowed the dog to catch the cat.
She swallowed the cat to catch the bird.
She swallowed the bird to catch the spider
that wiggled and wiggled and tickled
inside her.
She swallowed the spider to catch the fly.
But I don't know why she swallowed
that fly.
Perhaps she'll cry.

There was an old lady who swallowed
a horse.
She cried, "Wait! A horse?"
She didn't, of course.

There Was an Old Lady

World (West African)
Musical Youth Productions

Verse 1

1. There was an old lady who swallowed a fly. I don't know why she swallowed the fly. Perhaps she'll cry.

Verse 2

2. There was an old lady who swallowed a spider that wiggled and wiggled and tickled inside her.

She swallowed the spider to catch the fly. I don't know why she swallowed the fly. Perhaps she'll cry.

Verse 3-8

3. There was an old lady who swallowed a bird. How absurd to swallow a bird!
4. There was an old lady who swallowed a cat. I imagine that! She swallowed a cat.
5. There was an old lady who swallowed a dog. My, what a hog, to swallow a dog.
6. There was an old lady who swallowed a goat— just opened her throat and swallowed a goat!
7. There was an old lady who swallowed a cow. I don't know how she swallowed a cow!

She swallowed the bird to catch the spider that wiggled and wiggled and tickled inside her.
She swallowed the cat to catch the bird.
She swallowed the dog to catch the cat.
She swallowed the goat to catch the dog.
She swallowed the cow to catch the goat.

She swallowed the spider to catch the fly. I don't know why she swallowed the fly. Perhaps she'll cry.

Verse 8

There was an old lady who swallowed a horse.

She cried, "Wait! A horse?"
She didn't, of course.

23

GLOSSARY

absurd—silly or foolish

gulped—eaten quickly without much chewing

swallowed—moved from the mouth to the stomach

GUIDED READING ACTIVITIES

1. What did the old lady swallow first? How many animals did she swallow?

2. The old lady swallowed a goat. What part of your body rhymes with goat? Can you think of other words that rhyme with goat?

3. Which animal was your favorite? Draw a picture of it.

TO LEARN MORE

Colandro, Lucille. *There Was an Old Lady Who Swallowed Some Books!* New York: Cartwheel-Scholastic, 2012.

Holmes, Jeremy. *There Was an Old Lady Who Swallowed a Fly.* San Francisco: Chronicle Books, 2009.

Ward, Jennifer. *There Was an Old Monkey Who Swallowed a Frog.* New York: Marshall Cavendish, 2010.